Sports Jokes

Joe King

Abdo Kids Junior
is an Imprint of Abdo Kids
abdobooks.com

abdobooks.com

Published by Abdo Kids, a division of ABDO, P.O. Box 398166, Minneapolis, Minnesota 55439.
Copyright © 2022 by Abdo Consulting Group, Inc. International copyrights reserved in all countries.
No part of this book may be reproduced in any form without written permission from the publisher.
Abdo Kids Junior™ is a trademark and logo of Abdo Kids.

Printed in the United States of America, North Mankato, Minnesota.

102021

012022

THIS BOOK CONTAINS
RECYCLED MATERIALS

Photo Credits: Getty Images, Shutterstock

Production Contributors: Teddy Borth, Jennie Forsberg, Grace Hansen

Design Contributors: Candice Keimig, Pakou Moua

Library of Congress Control Number: 2021940306

Publisher's Cataloging-in-Publication Data

Names: King, Joe, author.
Title: Sports jokes / by Joe King
Description: Minneapolis, Minnesota : Abdo Kids, 2022 | Series: Abdo kids jokes | Includes online resource.
Identifiers: ISBN 9781098209216 (lib. bdg.) | ISBN 9781644946350 (pbk.) | ISBN 9781098209919 (ebook)
    | ISBN 9781098260279 (Read-to-Me ebook)
Subjects: LCSH: Jokes--Juvenile literature. | Wit and humor--Juvenile literature. | Sports--Juvenile
    literature.
Classification: DDC 818.602--dc23

Table of Contents

Sports Jokes 4

Joke-Telling Tips!. . . .22

Glossary. 23

Index 24

Abdo Kids Code. 24

Sports Jokes

Why was it so windy

inside the sports arena?

All the fans!

What is harder to catch

the faster you run?

Your breath!

4

OH!
HA!
Why do porcupines always win the game?
They have the most points.
DID I WIN?
5

What did the coach say to the broken vending machine?

I want my quarter back!

What state do football players go to when they need a new uniform?

New Jersey.

What is a cheerleader's favorite food?
Cheerios!
Y-U-M!
GO BREAKFAST GO!

What do you call a pig who plays basketball?

A ball hog!

Why did the basketball player bring his suitcase on the court?

Because he traveled a lot!

Why do basketball players love cookies?
Because they can dunk them!
SLAM DUNK!

What runs around a baseball field but never moves?

A fence!

Where do catchers sit at lunch?

Behind the plate.

HA!
What's the one rule zebras follow in baseball?
Three stripes and you're out!
HOW many stripes do I have?!
11

When is a baseball player
like a spider?

When he catches a fly ball!

What animal is best at
hitting a baseball?

A bat!

12

Did you hear the joke about the pop fly?
Never mind. It's way over your head.
THE JOKE
YOU

Why is tennis such a loud
sport?

The players cause a racket!

Why did the golfer wear
two pairs of pants?

In case she got a hole in one!

14

Why couldn't the ballerina stop dancing?
Because it was tutu fun!
and SPIN!
and TWIRL!
and TWIST!
and POSE!
15

What kind of dinosaur

can you ride in a rodeo?

A Bronco-saurus!

What is a delivery driver's

favorite sport?

Boxing.

16

What is a boxer's favorite drink?

Fruit punch!

POW!
GULP!

Why are hockey rinks rounded?

Why can't Cinderella play soccer?

18

Why did the chicken get a **penalty**?
For fowl play.
That joke was eggs-cellent!
You're a real comedi-hen.

What is a sheep's

favorite game?

Baaaaa-dminton!

What is an elf's

favorite sport?

North Pole vaulting.

How did the baseball glove say goodbye to the ball?

I'll catch you later!

GOOD LUCK!

SEE YOU SOON!

Joke-Telling Tips!

- Know your audience

- Timing is everything

- Confidence is key

- Go out on a high note!

Glossary

penalty
a punishment given in sports to a player or team that breaks a rule.

pun
a joke using a word that sounds like a different word or has another meaning. Examples from this book are "fowl" (foul) and "stripes" (strikes).

Index

animals 5, 8, 11, 12, 16, 19, 20

baseball 10, 11, 12, 13, 21

basketball 8, 9

boxing 16, 17

cheerleading 7

coach 6

dance 15

fans 4

food 6, 7, 10

football 6

golf 14

hockey 18

rodeo 16

soccer 18

tennis 14

Visit **abdokids.com** to access crafts, games, videos, and more!